MRS. D'SOUZA'S DISPUTE WITH GOD

A SHORT STORY

ANITHA KRISHNAN

DREAM PEDLAR BOOKS

For Kala Maami & Sekhar Chitappa,
you paved the path to paradise.
The Gods are lucky to have you in their midst.

For Abhinav,
you transform our lives into paradise.

For Dhruv,
you are paradise itself.

ABOUT THIS BOOK

Mrs. D'Souza's Dispute with God

Two things were annoying Mrs. D'Souza. One, the fact that she was dead. And second, the line of dead folks waiting to meet their Maker was insufferably long and impossibly docile.

Restless and teeming with questions, she decides to take matters in her own hands and sets out to find God. Not a big deal, really.

Except for one small thing. How do you seek someone when you don't even know what they look like?

1

─────────

DEATH

Mrs. D'Souza was not at all happy about the fact that she had just died.

She had only been going about her usual grocery run, making her way back home on her trusty TVS Scooty, bags of groceries neatly wedged between her feet on the platform, when one of those BMW sedans with tinted windows burst out of nowhere and careened into her sideways, dragging her, her trusted mount, and her bags of carefully chosen groceries for quite a distance.

Of course, it then sped away without a moment's hesitation, which is why the driver didn't notice how the *pallu* end of Mrs. D'Souza's new cotton *saree*, a light pink and floral affair for the end of summer, had caught on one of the BMW's wheels and had dragged her along, disrobing her alongside killing her.

At a safe distance away from the scene of the incident, the driver stopped, ripped the dawn pink shreds of the saree out of the wheels as much as he could, and deposited his car at an acquaintance's garage for a thorough repair and cleaning. The acquaintance asked no questions; he was paid more than enough to do what was required without prying into details unnecessary and irrelevant to him.

At the time of her death and for a few moments afterwards, Mrs. D'Souza was not entirely aware of all that had transpired.

She only worried that her beloved Scooty was ruined because she couldn't afford a loan for a new one right now, not on her primary schoolteacher's salary, not when she was still saving up for her children's college fees. She was also annoyed that her groceries were ruined and that she wouldn't be able to make her Sunday special for the family dinner. *Paav bhaji.*

And surprisingly, she was no longer at the crowded intersection she had been only moments ago.

The stench of petrol, exhaust fumes and roadside garbage that had mingled with the sickly sweet scent of people's squashed hopes and budding desires no longer tickled her nose. She noticed it only by its absence.

Gone also were the countless vehicles and irate drivers, the blaring horns and the clang of bells from a nearby temple that never failed to remind her to seek the divine even amid the chaos and commotion of day-to-day life.

Where moments ago there had been a leaden sky, darker than the grey asphalt of the road and threatening to burst open at any instant, was now a vast expanse of blue sky far above her head and green grass below her feet. It was as if she had fallen into an Enid Blyton book, and an adventure was just lurking around the corner, simply waiting to happen.

A long line of people snaked in front of her, and Mrs. D'Souza found herself standing at the end of it. She stepped to the side to see where the line led, but it was too long and too circuitous. And she was too short to be able to see above the towering heads of the people who stood in front of her.

"Excuse me," a voice said just as Mrs. D'Souza felt a tap on her lower back.

She spun around. Where there had been no one only a few seconds ago, now stood at least a dozen other people, each looking around in confusion. Even as she watched, more and more people appeared out of nowhere and kept joining the line.

"Excuse me, Ma'am," the voice said again, and this time Mrs. D'Souza looked down to see a young girl peering up into her eyes.

With her schoolteacher's eye, Mrs. D'Souza appraised the child in a quick second. The girl was dressed in a pale yellow frock with a meadow of bluebells embroidered close to the hem. Her feet were clad in brown Bata sandals, standard fare for children from middle-class families. Her waist-length black hair was oiled and neatly tied in two plaits with yellow ribbons. A little black *bindi* was pressed to the centre of her forehead.

Children presented a familiar ground to Mrs. D'Souza. Besides, something about this child and her orderly appearance was extremely endearing for two reasons.

First, it was so rare to come across such a well-groomed and well-mannered child. And second, the familiar company of a child was something Mrs. D'Souza could hold on to and draw immense courage from in this time of great confusion and chaos.

So she squatted on her haunches until she was at eye-level with the girl. "Yes, love?"

"Where are we, Ma'am?" the child asked. (She had a gaping hole where her top two front teeth ought to have been. She could have been no older than six or seven, that lovely age when they were still innocent but also quite grown up.)

"I don't know," Mrs. D'Souza sighed and stood up. "But let's find out, shall we?"

The girl gave a hint of a smile and nodded her head vigorously.

Holding the child's hand, Mrs. D'Souza stepped out of the line and drew level with the person ahead of her.

"Excuse me, *bhai sahib*?" Mrs. D'Souza began.

It was an old man in a white *kurta pyjama*. His thick mop of white hair was tousled and his rimless spectacles sat askew on top of his nose. He looked as if he had just been roused from a deep slumber and was still thinking about the last tendrils of his dream slipping away from conscious memory into his subconscious.

Mrs. D'Souza doubted she'd be able to coax any useful answers out of him but, for someone who made snap judgements about people, she was surprisingly not prone to jumping to conclusions about them without first giving them a chance to prove otherwise.

"Do you know where we are?" she asked him.

With the palm of his hand, the man gestured at her to wait. With the frustrating slowness of motion that seemed to afflict older human beings, he then slipped his hand into the pocket of his *kurta* from where he drew a hearing aid and plugged it into his ear. He fixed his spectacles and peered at her closely.

Mrs. D'Souza waited with the unassailable patience she had come to acquire over the years through her endless interactions with large crowds of small children, up to fifty or sixty in a class, each wild and wonderful in their own unique ways.

"Yes, Ma'am," the old man said, as though resuming a conversation after a brief pause, "please tell me now. What were you saying? I'm deaf as a stone without my hearing aid. But … that's really a strange choice of words, isn't it? Deaf as a stone? Off late, I've begun to wonder why. You seem like you would know. Are you a schoolteacher? Or perhaps you work in a bank?"

Mrs. D'Souza was impressed. She had written off this man as nothing but an old cuckoo head at first, but with the right implements to aid him, he was proving that he could observe and discern the world around him almost as well as she could.

But before she could answer, the man squatted down quite like she had and smiled at the little girl who still held Mrs. D'Souza's hand.

"Hello, lovely child," the man said. "What is your name?"

"Neela," the child replied in a small voice.

"What a beautiful name!"

"It means blue. Sapphire blue."

"How old are you?"

"I am six years and eight months old."

"*Arrey waah!* Your birthday must be coming up soon. When is it?"

"October 20."

"We share the same birthdate," Mrs. D'Souza said with delight, and the child gave her a small grin.

"Very good, *beta*!" The old man smiled at her indulgently, then dropped his voice to a mock-whisper. "Would you like to see some magic?"

Neela nodded. Mrs. D'Souza was yet to come across a child who wouldn't be lured by magic or puppies or treats.

The man waved an empty hand in front of Neela's face, then ran it above and over the child's head and behind her ear and presented a closed fist to her.

"Is there anything in here?"

"No." Neela shook her head.

"Are you sure?"

"Yes, I'm sure."

"Are you really, really sure?" the man asked again, his voice rising higher and higher with each question, teasing gently like an indulgent grandparent.

"Ya?" This time, Neela's response was not as certain as her previous ones had been.

"Ta-ta-da-ta-daaaaaa!" With great flourish, the man opened his fist. In the palm of his hand lay a small bar of Cadbury 5 star!

Mrs. D'Souza's mouth began to water at the sight of her favourite chocolate, reminding her it is was probably way past dinner time and … hadn't she been going home with groceries? Everything came rushing back to her in that instant. Everything that she had forgotten for a few moments, mesmerized by this gentleman's magic trick.

A small tug on her hand made her look down, and Mrs. D'Souza saw Neela look up with a questioning gaze. It took her a moment to comprehend that the child was waiting for her permission to take the chocolate offered by the man.

"Sure, Neela!" Mrs. D'Souza said. She was elated that the child had exercised caution before accepting a treat from a stranger. Yet, the way the child had looked up at her for permission had also left her feeling surprisingly sad, as though someone had denied *her* a treat that she would have loved.

Neela grabbed the chocolate from the old man's palm, as though afraid it would disappear by the very magic that had brought it into existence. "Thank you," she said, and promptly put it into a cleverly concealed pocket in her dress.

"Don't you wish to eat it now?" Mrs. D'Souza asked her.

The child shook her head. "I'm saving it for later."

"Sounds like a sensible thing to do," the old man said. He raised his palm for a hi-five and the child happily obliged.

He then drew himself back up to standing and turned to Mrs. D'Souza once more. "Yes, Ma'am. Forgive that brief interlude. I can't help but show off my magical talents whenever I see little kids. They seem to be the only appreciative audience. And from where I come, I don't see many of them often enough."

"Are you talking about your grandchildren?" Mrs. D'Souza asked.

The old man's eyes misted over, but he merely nodded and said nothing. Clearly, it was a touchy subject.

"Er … excuse me," Neela said much to the relief of the old man and Mrs. D'Souza. "But does anybody know where we are?"

"Oh, yes! That's what we had come to ask you about," Mrs. D'Souza chimed in merrily.

"Oh!" The old man looked from Mrs. D'Souza to Neela and back at Mrs. D'Souza again. Confusion clouded his face. But when he spoke, it was with great compassion and sorrow.

"I thought you knew," he said. "Why! We are at the place where people go when they die."

2

―――――

DENIAL

Are you out of your mind, you senile old fool? was the first thought that popped into Mrs. D'Souza head.

In fact, the thought was so emphatic in her head it was almost as if someone had shouted it out loud.

But she had the presence of mind to not blurt it out aloud. Years of working as a schoolteacher had trained her in the art of keeping her mouth shut when she all she wanted to do was lambaste the person in front of her.

Eventually, when she opened her mouth to speak, at first she could do little other than open and close, open and close it, like a fish in water.

"It cannot … that's not pos… that's ridiculous!" she managed to say at last.

And then she looked down at Neela and back at the old man, realizing for the first time that if what the old man had said was true, then they too were dead.

The old man nodded, comprehending the words she said and the ones she was unable to bring herself to say. "It's hard to accept it at first," he said. "It takes a little time. A little getting used to."

Mrs. D'Souza found herself shaking her head. "No." Her breath grew jagged and noisy. "No … NoNoNoNoNo! Stop talking nonsense! I don't believe you."

"Shh!" someone shushed. Mrs. D'Souza looked around but tears had sprung into her eyes and clouded her vision. She wiped them away hastily to find the people ahead of and behind the old man in the line staring at her, watching the spectacle she was becoming.

"What are you staring at? Mind your own business," she barked in their general direction. "Assholes!" she threw in for good measure. Beside her, Neela winced.

"Well, if we're really dead, it doesn't fucking matter, does it? We can shout and scream, swear and curse, and we'd still be fucking dead!" Mrs. D'Souza screamed at no one in particular.

Neela pulled her hand away from Mrs. D'Souza's and went and stood beside the old man, clasping her hand around his gnarled little finger. He patted her on the head and then, turning back to Mrs. D'Souza, said, "My dear! It is very upsetting news indeed. Why don't we take a seat for a bit? It'll help you calm down."

He gestured somewhere behind her but Mrs. D'Souza didn't care to look. She shook her head wildly. Clutching the *pallu* of her *saree*, she began to knead and wring it in her hands. "No, no, no! You don't understand. I have to get back home. My children and my husband are waiting for me. I need to make dinner. A new school year begins tomorrow. I'm teaching English to the 4th standard children, you see. Such an important year for them. Nine- and ten-year-olds. They need a good, experienced teacher, but also a kind one. Do you know how rare it is to find someone like that?"

She looked down at the hem of her saree and the tips of her sandal-clad feet peeking out from under it. Only that morning she had been to the beauty parlour for a mani-pedi and had opted for a very pale pink nail polish; it was almost colourless.

The students were not permitted to wear makeup at school. Mrs. D'Souza had been of the firm belief that only if the teachers and staff followed the rules could they expect the children to follow suit.

But the principal, Mrs. Mathur, that vixen with her bright red lipstick and permed hair and high heels was hardly a role model. Mrs. D'Souza, despite her high ideals and moral values, felt pale and washed out in the presence of the principal and had settled for at least a mani-pedi and a facial before the school year was scheduled to begin.

A pang of regret surged through her. She could have spent the last day of the summer holidays with her own children, teenagers though they were and had opted to hang out with their friends at the neighbourhood mall. She should have insisted more on family time. She should have.

She looked up at the old man and said, "What children need the most is kindness, not knowledge. They love me, you know, all the students at the school. I've never believed in scolding or shaming them."

Then she knelt down in front of Neela and held her shoulders. Looking into the child's beautiful black eyes, she pleaded, "Please forgive me, dear child. I don't know what had come over me earlier. I was completely in the wrong. I had no business yelling and cursing the way I did. I am very sorry,

Neela. Can you please find it in your beautiful heart to forgive me? Please?"

Neela nodded without hesitation. "Yes. I can forgive. But … but I don't know how to. Can you please show me how to do that, Ma'am?"

Mrs. D'Souza burst into tears then. "You're not mad at me anymore, are you?"

"No."

"Are you afraid of me?"

Neela hesitated, then shook her head slowly. "No."

"Can I please give you a hug then?"

Neela nodded, and Mrs. D'Souza wrapped the child in an embrace. When she drew back, Neela wiped the tears from her cheeks. "It's OK to cry," the child said.

Mrs. D'Souza gave her a wet smile. "Thank you! Your forgiveness means a lot to me."

Her heart now freed of an enormous burden, resolve surged through her. She stood up and asked the old man. "Who told you we're all dead here?"

He shrugged. "I can feel it in my bones. Can't you tell?"

"I don't feel any different than I did when I was riding back home with the groceries. I'm going to go ahead and find out where this line leads, what we're all queuing up for anyway."

"To meet our maker, of course!" Neela piped up, looking strangely elated.

"Do you feel it in your bones too? That you're dead?" Mrs. D'Souza asked.

Neela pouted her lips as if in thought, then said, "No. But then we can't feel anything when we're dead, can we?"

"Who told you that?"

"My mother. When *Aaji* died, I tried to wake her up. But my mother told me that *Aaji* can't feel anything anymore, and so I should stop patting her cheeks or tapping her shoulders to wake her up."

"I see."

"But later that night *Aaji* came in my dreams and said she'd always be with me. I told mother about it the next day, and she shooed me away, told me to stop lying. But I wasn't lying."

"I know you weren't lying," Mrs. D'Souza said. "Sometimes grown-ups find it hard to believe the things that children know naturally."

"Is that why you're finding it hard to believe you're dead?" Neela asked.

Mrs. D'Souza was taken aback. The girl wasn't trying to be impertinent but her remark was incisive, even if unwittingly so.

"Perhaps," Mrs. D'Souza answered as honestly as she could. She didn't wish to insult the young child's intelligence. "But I'm still going to go and see if God is really waiting to meet us at the head of the line. I need proof."

"I'll come with you," Neela said, skipping towards Mrs. D'Souza excitedly.

"It might be a long walk."

"That's OK. We can all go together. Uncle can show us some more magic tricks. And I can share my 5-star with you two when we feel hungry."

Neela's assumptions that the three of them had now become a group were endearing, yet Mrs. D'Souza needed to ask the old man, "You sure you'd like to come along?"

"Absolutely!" He grinned. "I have nowhere else to be."

3

———

DESPAIR

The grass under their feet was lush and velvety. It made walking effortless. The sky was blue and bright although there was no visible sun. The air was cool on their skin although there was no breeze.

Mrs. D'Souza inhaled deeply. The air was crisp and fresh with a faint aroma of roses and jasmines, but above all the sanctifying scent of sandalwood drifted her way. It was the ubiquitous perfume of worship in her city. Mumbai.

Truth be told, she would have liked to walk alone for a bit, left to herself and her thoughts, without having to look after Neela or put up with the old man's insistence that they were all dead.

Yet, she was glad for their company, albeit at a slight distance. They walked a few steps behind her, the man regaling Neela with tricks and treats, the child telling him silly jokes and sending him into peals of laughter.

The people standing in the line turned to look at them as they passed. Occasionally, Mrs. D'Souza stopped to chat with someone in the line and inquire if they knew what was going

13

on. The responses were the same. Either they didn't know and, unlike her, didn't mind not knowing, or they believed they were all dead and waiting to meet their Maker.

But the most surprising thing of all was that not one person tried to stop her from advancing. Not one person asked her to go back and queue up instead of trying to get ahead of the others in the line. That alone was proof enough that she was no longer in sultry Mumbai but somewhere else entirely.

In all her life, Mrs. D'Souza had never seen such an orderly line. There was no jostling or pushing, no shoving or bickering. No one seemed to have any questions either. Nor did anyone seem to be in a hurry. It was almost as if they were in some kind of a stupor.

There were all kinds of people here. Not only from all corners of India, but from everywhere across the world, it seemed.

Quite a few were dressed like ascetics, in the fiery colours of saffron, yellow, or maroon.

Some chanted *shlokas*. Some whispered the names of gods under their breath. Some raised their hands to the blue sky above while some others knelt and pressed their foreheads to the ground.

It was like walking in a dream where time and space had ceased to exist. There was nothing but green grass and blue skies as far as the eye could see.

"We must have been walking for hours now," Mrs. D'Souza turned around and said to the old man, who was now playing hopscotch with Neela.

"You don't say," he said without looking up at her. His

breath was a little short from the exertion. "It feels like we've only just begun."

"What do you mean?"

"We're back at where we started." He pointed to the line and sure enough, Mrs. D'Souza found herself staring into the faces of the people who had witnessed her foul-mouthed outburst earlier.

"How can that be?" Mrs. D'Souza could hear the shrillness creep into her voice again. With great effort, she tried to quell it. "As far as I could tell, we've been walking in a straight line—"

"For an infinitely long time," Neela piped up, continuing to hop on invisible squares on the grass.

Mrs. D'Souza looked at the child incredulously. "Surely that's out of syllabus for you?"

Neela, standing on one leg in mid-hop, puffed out her chest with pride and said, "My older brother taught me about circles and tangents. He is in 4th standard."

"Well done!" the old man said with glee. He was almost about to clap his hands but stopped when he saw the look of frustration on Mrs. D'Souza's face and made to rub his hands instead.

But instead of erupting with frustration, Mrs. D'Souza asked thoughtfully, "How will we ever get to the head of the line … this circle-line then?"

"We'll have to wait for our turn, like everyone else," the old man said.

"But that's ridiculous! We should at least be told what's going on. Whoever hauled us here can't simply expect us to keep standing and waiting for as long as they please!"

Mrs. D'Souza couldn't stand not knowing what was in

store for her. She had a home to get back to. A family that was waiting for her, even if it was her culinary skills and the *paav bhaji* they cared more about than her presence.

"At this rate, when will we get to meet God," she wrung her hands in despair, "if that's truly who's waiting at the end of the line?"

"Why do we have to go in search of God? What if we called him here?" Neela piped up again, now straddling two squares, earning another look of wonder and disbelief from Mrs. D'Souza.

"Why! That's a brilliant idea! You must be the topper of your class!" Mrs. D'Souza said.

"No. I don't like to study for exams. That's boring," the girl said with a nonchalant shrug that irked the schoolteacher in Mrs. D'Souza, who couldn't believe her hears.

"Boring?" she shrieked. "But what will you do when you have to appear for the Board exams? Your marks will determine your future."

Neela looked at Mrs. D'Souza for a moment, then said, "That's not something I have to worry about now, do I?"

She resumed her game, leaving Mrs. D'Souza to watch her, mouth agape with incredulity. Whatever happened to the quiet, timid persona that Neela had exhibited when she had joined the queue right behind Mrs. D'Souza? It was as if the child's personality was undergoing a massive change in this place. The longer they stayed here, the more vocal she was becoming.

Which ought to have been a good thing, but the fact that Neela seemed to grow more and more at ease with her surroundings felt like some kind of betrayal to Mrs. D'Souza. She felt as if she were the last person standing.

"So, how do we call God here?" Mrs. D'Souza posed the question to Neela. The girl was clearly on a roll now, coming up with unexpected answers. But for once, she was quiet. She hopped for a while in silence while Mrs. D'Souza waited, correctly interpreting the girl's lack of speech as absorption in deep thought.

All of a sudden, without warning, Neela stopped, put her hands around her mouth and hollered, "Hello, God! Are you there? Mrs. D'Souza would like to have a word with you!"

The girl was full of surprises. The old man chuckled, which earned him a glare from Mrs. D'Souza, and he pretended to cough into his fist instead.

Nothing happened. No one appeared. Not God. Nor anyone else.

Only a handful of people in the line turned around to look at them momentarily, the spectacle they had become ever since their arrival at this strange place.

"Well?" Mrs. D'Souza said at last. "Where's He?"

"How do you know it's a He? God could be a She as well," Neela tut-tutted.

Mrs. D'Souza resisted the temptation to roll her eyes. She was still a teacher, after all, and she was habituated to holding herself to very high standards of behaviour, even if no one else expected her to.

"God could be gender-neutral too," she said.

"Good point," Neela said. "We'll have to ask God when God shows up." She shrugged, then resumed her game of hopscotch, as if it was the only important activity for now and there were no other pressing concerns.

With a sigh, Mrs. D'Souza turned towards the old man.

"Well, Sir! Do *you* have any ideas for beckoning God to our aid?"

The old man scratched his jaw, then said, "Isn't that what prayer is for?"

He put his palms together, closed his eyes, and began to chant softly.

Hare Ram, Hare Ram
Ram Ram Hare Hare
Hare Krishna, Hare Krishna
Krishna Krishna Hare Hare

He opened one eye, then another, in a way that made Neela giggle. Then he made a big show of looking here and there and everywhere. "Oops! No God again." He shrugged and creased his face into a concerned frown, and even though he may have resorted to theatrics to lighten her mood, Mrs. D'Souza found the entire drama agonizing.

"It's your turn now," Neela said to Mrs. D'Souza, who only shook her head, then walked away from the old man and the young girl, away from the circular line of supposedly dead souls waiting to meet their maker.

She could hear Neela protesting in the background, saying "Not fair," and the old man assuaging her, no doubt, although Mrs. D'Souza could no longer discern his words.

When she had put sufficient distance between them and herself—not that she cared to turn around and check, but the fact that she could see no one out of the corners of her eyes was assurance enough—she sank to the plush grass and stared at the horizon. Seeing, yet not seeing anything.

When was the last time she had prayed?

Oh, she did go through the motions at school, standing up and folding her hands and closing her eyes along with all the other staff and children three times a day—during the morning assembly, right before lunch break, and at the end of the day right before dismissal—while the chosen student recited the prayer for the occasion over the speaker system for the entire school to hear. That didn't count.

She had long stopped going to Sunday church and had resisted all temptation to impose her ideologies of God, faith and religion on her children. Her husband, being an atheist, had been quite content to follow suit.

If she were to call out now, would God respond? When was the last time she had called out to God? The answer came to her promptly, as if it had there all along and had only been waiting for the question to be asked.

The last time she had prayed, she was a few weeks shy of turning seven. That was when her mother had died in an accident.

She too had been on her way back home from the weekly market, having set in motion preparations for her daughter's upcoming birthday.

Mrs. D'Souza's mother had wanted to get a beautiful party frock stitched for her little girl. An October child, her birthday fell smack in the midst of the festive season. Dussehra. Diwali. Christmas. All the good tailors were booked weeks in advance, and Mrs. D'Souza's mother had been among the first customers to place their order in the beginning of September.

The tailor had promised that the birthday child's party frock would be ready at least a fortnight before her big day. Mission accomplished, Mrs. D'Souza's mother had been making her way back home in high spirits that even Mumbai's monsoon downpour couldn't dampen.

All it took was a single misstep into an overflowing pothole. She lost her balance and fell away from the pavement on to the road, where an auto rickshaw had slammed into her.

It hadn't been the rickshaw driver's fault either. He had been driving slowly in the rain, and there was nothing he could do except brake the instant he saw a figure fell unannounced in front of his vehicle. It wasn't soon enough.

Of course, Mrs. D'Souza hadn't learnt of these details until years later. At the tender age of six and three-quarters, she was only told that her mother had gone away to live with God and that the only way the child could see her mother again was when the time came for her too to go and live with God.

Her almost-seven-year-old self had spent countless nights calling out to God.

"God, is my mommy with you?"

"God, may I please come and live with you and mommy?"

"God, is mommy happy?"

"God, can you please take me to mommy?"

"God, why don't you answer me?"

"God, can you please ask mommy to come and visit me?"

Eventually she had found it difficult to keep asking questions when answers were not forthcoming. And she had stopped calling out to God altogether.

4

DELIVERANCE

God. The word was strange and alien inside her mouth. It was hard and harsh, now that she thought about it. Not soft and comforting. Not like Mommy.

Maybe that was the trouble. God should have been a woman. Calm and kind and gentle. Like her mother had been, or whatever little Mrs. D'Souza remembered of her mother, which was hardly anything.

She couldn't remember what her mother had looked like, even though there were several photos of her. She couldn't remember what her mother had looked like in real life. She had no memory of her mother's scent nor of her touch.

What she remembered of her mother was a presence. One was that kind and compassionate, warm and safe.

Surely, the presence of God too should feel that way, shouldn't it? God didn't have to look like Dumblebore or Gandalf, old and wise and all-knowing.

But then, she didn't want God to look like a pretty woman either, fingernails dripping scarlet red paint, feet clad in too high heels, and a smile that reeked of strength and power but failed to evoke trust.

Frustrated with the images that kept popping up in her head, Mrs. D'Souza looked up at the blue sky and called out, "So what do you really look like, God?"

A silver fork of lightning cleaved the sky swiftly but quietly. It was like a momentary flash of silver in an already bright sky.

Mrs. D'Souza turned around to face the line of souls but no one seemed to have noticed a thing. Neela seemed to have stopped playing hopscotch and was watching the old man instead, who was moving his hands in the air as though he were juggling or performing a magic trick.

She turned back and—

"Aaah!" Mrs. D'Souza shrieked and tumbled backwards, her hand on her chest, but her heart had already leapt into her mouth.

In front of her stood a blue person.

"Surprise!" The person smiled at her. In that instant, Mrs. D'Souza's fear and shock ebbed away and she was filled with an unexpected sense of joy and well-being.

"Who are you? And where did you come from?" she asked, already knowing that the answers didn't really matter somehow.

The blue person smiled. "You wanted to see what I looked like, didn't you?"

It occurred to Mrs. D'Souza that perhaps this was God, perhaps it wasn't, but she no longer needed any confirmation. She knew. Somehow she knew.

This God who stood in front of her was tall and strong, but also graceful and beautiful. This God had black curly locks of hair that fell to their shoulders and even though there was no breeze, this God's curls and robes swayed and swirled around their form.

This God reminded Mrs. D'Souza of the first time she had made a best friend, the first time she had fallen in love, and the first time she had held her oldest child as a newborn in her arms.

"Why! You look just like a Bollywood hero," Mrs. D'Souza shrieked with delight, having found a suitable answer at last.

For surely, this God was easily the son every mother wanted, the brother every young girl looked up to, and the lover every young woman yearned for. A perfect combination of strength and grace, of power and beauty, of mischief and charisma.

The blue God threw their head back and laughed, and that made Mrs. D'Souza happy.

But, at the same time, this God was not really male. Nor female either. The more she looked, the less she could discern. And that threw her into confusion again.

"Not really," she said, more to herself than to the blue God in front of her. "Not exactly a Bollywood hero."

"I am beyond all labels," the God said. Their voice was as deep as an ocean's roar yet as sweet as a koel's call. "I am in every name, yet no single name describes me wholly."

"Is that why you don't come when we call you? Because we're using all the wrong names?" The memory of an unresolved grief gripped Mrs. D'Souza's heart.

"How can I come when I've never left?" the blue God said enigmatically.

Mrs. D'Souza's eyes filled with tears and her chest swelled with a love and a longing that couldn't possibly coexist.

"B... but ... it ... never ... never felt ... that way," she hiccuped through sobs. "Ever since ... you took my mother away, I've been so alone ... so lonely."

She looked up sharply with an anger that had been festering in her all along, an anger that morphed and hardened from grief and anxiety and desperation over the years. "Why did you take her away from me? Why couldn't you have waited?"

The blue God tilted his head at her questioningly. "Until when?"

"Until when?" Mrs. D'Souza shook her fist in the God's face as if this was the most absurd question she had ever been asked in her entire lifetime. "Until when? I don't know. Until I was older? Until she had lived to a ripe old age? I have no clue. How am I supposed to know that? But definitely not before my seventh birthday. That was a low blow."

The blue God only smiled at her with such compassion that the very next instant, Mrs. D'Souza found her anger dissipate. It no longer squeezed her chest in a vise-like grip.

"It is the way of life," the blue God said. "To live. To die. Never at a predetermined time as perceived by mortal eyes."

Mrs. D'Souza understood. "There is never a right time, is there?"

Now that anger and grief no longer clouded her vision, she observed the blue God with greater attention. They were mostly unadorned, except for a pair of chunky gold earrings that clung to their earlobes and a gold bracelet on each wrist. They held no flute in one hand, nor a conch in the other. No peacock feather adorned their luscious locks.

Yet the God shone with a brilliance, with a light that was warmer yet more tender than that of the sun and the moon and all the stars put together. Behind the God, the blue sky and the green grass sparkled as if lit by the summer sun.

In that moment of clarity, Mrs. D'Souza remembered what she had wanted to meet God for. "Am I dead?" she asked. "Is it true that we've all lined up here to meet you?"

The God's eyes twinkled. For the first time since she had arrived in this in-between place, this waiting room of sorts, she didn't fear the answer to that question.

"Life. Death. These too are mere labels, aren't they?"

"I'd still like to know," Mrs. D'Souza said, worried she might be sounding very petty in the presence of this magnificent God. Yet, she didn't feel the need to hide what her heart truly felt.

"What do you feel?" the God asked. "Alive? Or dead?"

Mrs. D'Souza was taken aback by that question. She had never considered that before. Even after being transported to this place, she had carried on being her own inquisitive self, determined to find out where she was and what was happening around her.

"Truth be told, I don't feel any different than when I was … alive. But …" She looked around her, at this placid landscape, at the kind old man and Neela, still bantering and playing with each other, at the long line of people waiting to reach some unknown destination, yet unperturbed and in no rush. "It's this place that feels different and strange. Surreal. As if this is all a dream."

The blue God chuckled. "Perhaps it all is," they said mysteriously. "That doesn't make it any less real."

Mrs. D'Souza turned back to face the blue God in alarm. "Now I'm worried. What if I were to open my eyes and wake up and you're gone, and all this has disappeared? I don't think I'd be able to bear it."

"That would give you a chance to cook your Sunday dinner special for your family," the blue God said, watching her closely.

Mrs. D'Souza blinked. It took her a few moments to recall the life she had left behind, the last thing she had been thinking of. *Paav bhaji.* Her beloved Scooty now just another indistinguishable chunk of metal at a scrapyard.

She imagined her family, huddled in the kitchen, calling her mobile phone repeatedly in vain, calling friends and neighbours to inquire about her whereabouts, worried and wondering why she hadn't come back home yet. Was the blue God really offering her a second chance at life?

As if reading her thoughts, the blue God said, "You could go back, if you wanted to."

Was it as simple as that? Mrs. D'Souza looked around again. "What about them?" she asked, pointing towards the old man and Neela. "What will happen to them? And to the others?" The schoolteacher in her would never permit her to leave a place until she was certain that everyone was in safe hands and taken care of.

The blue God looked at her with such tender love that Mrs. D'Souza knew instantly that her fears were misplaced.

"Why!" the blue God said. "Everything and everyone here is all that you ever longed for in every lifetime you spent on earth."

Neela, the almost-seven-year-old trying to make sense of death, was not unlike how Mrs. D'Souza had been as a young child herself.

The kind old man was the image of God Mrs. D'Souza had

unknowingly carried within her subconscious, a motherless child looking for a strong father-figure to steer her through grief and pain.

The blue sky and the green meadow had become Mrs. D'Souza's very definition of a happy place ever since she read her first Enid Blyton book at the age of six.

And the long orderly, patient line? Why! That neat orderliness, and its promise and reassurance of safety were all that Mrs. D'Souza had ever wanted whenever faced with the chaos of thoughts in her head or the commotion of the world outside.

And the blue being standing here was a God her heart had continued to call out to throughout her life even though she had ceased to utter the word out loud.

Understanding was a subtractive process, Mrs. D'Souza realized. The more she understood, the more answers she found, the more questions fell away from her mind like heavy rocks rolling down from a hilltop and disappearing into the bottom of an ocean, never to be seen again.

An invisible breeze tousled the blue God's curls again, and Mrs. D'Souza felt as if she would simply lift up and fly away wherever the blue God could take her, if only they'd ask her to come along.

"I no longer yearn for the things and the people I once craved for," she said.

The queue of longings dissipated behind her like florets of dandelion being blown away. Only the blue God remained standing on the green meadow under the blue sky.

"But now that I've found you, I can never leave you. I will not go away from you." Her heart ached with longing, but she was also strangely content, knowing what the blue God's next words would be.

The blue God smiled. Their lips were seductive, and Mrs. D'Souza knew she could spend eternity simply gazing into their black eyes.

"I am always with you," the blue God said, and their voice was the song of the Universe. "Wherever you go, there I am."

And Mrs. D'Souza understood that it didn't matter what she chose. She could go back to her life and live it as well as she could. Or she could move forth and find out what awaited her if she were to embrace her death.

It really didn't matter what she chose.

~ The End ~

Ready for more speculative fiction stories of Gods and humans? Dive into the touching tale of A Benevolent Goddess, who is punished for her desire to help human beings but is unable to find salvation by any other means.

ENJOYED MRS. D'SOUZA'S DISPUTE WITH GOD?

Thank you for reading *Mrs. D'Souza's Dispute with God*!

If you loved the story, I hope you will consider writing a short review—even a simple line or two—on the site where you bought the book.

Publishing is still driven by word of mouth, and when you leave a review it helps other readers decide this is a book worth reading. Thank you for your help in spreading the word.

You can also sign up to my monthly newsletter for updates on new book releases as well as heartfelt reflections on writing, reading, parenting and living the creative life.

Monthly Missives from The Dream Pedlar
https://thedreampedlar.com/newsletter

When you sign up, you will receive access to additional works of fiction available exclusively to subscribers.

AUTHOR'S NOTE

Dear Reader,

I wrote this short story more than a year ago in May 2023 when I was struggling to make progress on a speculative fiction novel (which I'm currently having great fun writing).

Back then, the character of Mrs. D'Souza appeared in my head as a formidable woman who was infuriated with God for the way death comes for people. Randomly. Illogically. Senselessly.

I had lost my maternal aunt in a tragic accident only a few months before that, and just last month a dear paternal uncle of mine, my father's youngest brother, passed away after his health took an unexpected turn for the worse.

Mrs. D'Souza was the character who could confront God and coax a reasonable response from him on the topic of death.

Writing her tale brought to mind some of the amazing teachers I was lucky enough to learn from during my mostly convent schooling in India.

It was an enriching experience that taught me to enter and

do the cross in a church with as much ease and faith as I'd experience going to a temple where I'd fold hands and bend down to touch my forehead to the ground in devotion.

Mrs. D'Souza is an amalgamation of all the amazing teachers who came into my life. Kind. Fiercely protective of her students. And always exhibiting great willingness to delve into topics 'outside of syllabus' but very pertinent to life. It is in this spirit that she has led this story.

And much like everyone who works with children, Mrs. D'Souza also exhibits the innocence of a child when it comes to matters of life and death that cannot be wholly or easily explained.

I don't even know her first name, like how I don't always remember or even know the first names of my teachers at school. They were always Ms. Rodrigues or Mrs. D'Lima or Sister Ferdinand, their last names serving as sufficient labels with which to address them.

Yet, those simple labels suffice today to bring back to memory the nurturing effect my teachers had on me and my peers. Among the ones I remember the most is Mrs. D'Lima, who taught me English in 10th standard at St. Felix Girls' High School in Pune, India. She nicknamed me 'Oxford' and I thrived academically under her encouragement.

Prior to that came Padmini Ma'am in Baroda, where I spent my 8th and 9th standards at Sabari Vidyalaya. Here we knew the first names of our teachers but not the last. She placed me several notches above the rest of the class in her assessment of my language skills. She taught us both English and Hindi, which was a rarity.

Oh, I could keep going down memory lane and write another book on this. But aren't we blessed when we can look back on our formative years and remember folks who nurtured our talents, who inspired and encouraged us to heights we couldn't even imagine back then?

Because even though I loved language and words and stories back then, I never thought that I'd be an author when I grew up. But now this phase of my life feels inevitable, as though I was headed this way all along.

Thank you for reading until the end. I hope you enjoyed the journey this book took you on and also reading the story behind the story.

We've come together so far. I'd love to stay in touch with you. And I hope you'd like to stay connected with me too.

I send out a monthly newsletter on the last Sunday of every month. Subscription is free.

You will be the first to hear of my forthcoming works. I also include updates on my writing life, book recommendations, free short fiction, and occasional surprises.

Thank you for staying with me this far. If you choose to accompany me further on this journey, I promise you a magical ride.

Climb aboard at https://thedreampedlar.com/newsletter!

~ Anitha Krishnan
Burlington, Ontario
8 February 2024

MORE BOOKS BY ANITHA KRISHNAN

https://thedreampedlar.com/books/

Dying Wishes

Finalist for 2023 Rakuten Kobo Emerging Writer Prize in Speculative Fiction category

A contemporary fantasy novel weaving Hindu mythology and South Indian folklore into a quest for belonging across different worlds — the World of Mortals and the World of Gods, India and Canada, the past and the present, the world outside and the one within.

Erased from Existence

A paranormal mystery in which a fifteen-year-old is erased from the memories and perception of everyone. Trapped in oblivion, she will have to unearth and reveal long-buried family secrets to escape.

The Land of No Reflection

A fantasy tale of two sightless young women on the run from their homeland, having committed the unpardonable crime of seeing.

A Benevolent Goddess

A story of a goddess who is punished for her desire to help human beings but is unable to find salvation by any other means.

In Search of Leo

A fantasy tale exploring the gamut of emotions that loss and grief can stir.

The Mind Meddler

A short fantasy story on the games The Mind Meddler plays by sneaking thoughts into people's minds, until he meets the one person who can resist his unkind mischief.

Hello, Dreamer! Poems & Dreams

An eclectic collection of 100 short poems encompassing musings on the universe and its mysteries, nature and human life, my secret longings and fears, love and heartbreak, the sun and the moon, the stars and the seas, light and shadow, and joy and nostalgia.

ABOUT THE AUTHOR

Anitha Krishnan is a speculative fiction author and an award-winning poet. Her fantasy novel, *Dying Wishes*, was a finalist for the 2023 Rakuten Kobo Emerging Writer Prize in the Speculative Fiction category.

She has lived in and left pieces of her heart in many places across the world including Singapore, Australia, Canada, and most of all in her beloved birthplace, India. She presently lives in Burlington, Ontario with her husband and their cherished child.

Find more books and her blog on the writing life at
https://thedreampedlar.com.

Sign up to her monthly newsletter at
https://thedreampedlar.com/newsletter
to receive heartfelt musings, exclusive updates, book recommendations, free fiction, and more!